This book
belongs to:

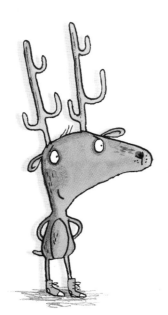

HOME

A house is made of
BOARDS and BEAMS
A home is made of
LOVE and DREAMS.
- anon.

Dedicated to my
grandparents,
Alice, Betty,
George and Sid,
for all your
love.

Papers used by Scholastic Children's Books are
made from wood grown in sustainable forests.

First published in 2009 by Scholastic Children's Books, Euston House, 24 Eversholt Street, London NW1 1DB, a division of Scholastic Ltd. www.scholastic.co.uk
...ciated companies worldwide. Text and illustrations copyright © 2009 Alex T. Smith. All rights reserved. The moral rights of Alex T. Smith have been asserted.

HB ISBN: 978 1407 10539 0   PB ISBN: 978 1407 10540 6

Printed in Singapore. 10 9 8 7 6 5 4 3 2

**SCHOLASTIC**

Once there was a house...

. . . A house that was a **home**.
And in the house that was a home
lived four best friends. They were called:
One, Two, Three and Four.

They lived happily
ever after, until . . .

One said, "Let's **all** move to somewhere different. We could be **pirates** and sail the seven seas!"

The others did **not** think this was a very good idea.

Two said,
     "I don't want to live on the sea!
It's far too **wet**. We should all live at the top
        of a mountain and learn to **yodel**!"
The others didn't think this was a good idea either.

Three sighed and said,
"I don't like heights!
Let's all live under the
ground in a dark, dark cave
and collect creepy-crawlies!"

This idea made
the others feel a
little bit itchy.

Four had other plans.
"All those ideas are silly!" he said in a
very bossy voice. "We should move to the
big city. . . and go to parties and
boogie-woogie all night long!"

The four friends didn't know what to do.
First they **talked**.

maybe...

an interesting point...

Then they **argued**.

Then they **fought**.

Finally they decided to go their separate wa

"If I'm going," they all shouted, "I'm taking the house with me!"

One took the door and
stormed off to the seaside.

Two took the walls and
stomped off up a mountain.

Three took the windows
and scurried off to a cave.

TO BIG CITY

Four picked up the floor and
shuffled away to the big city.

All that was left was the roof.

The four **not-at-all**-best friends
started their new lives
and were very happy . . . at first.

**One** became a pirate
and sailed the seas.

But the sea was much bigger and wetter than he had imagined.

And, worst of all, his **house** simply wasn't a **home** when it was just a door.

Two learned how to yodel.

She yodelled and yodelled.
But all she got back was an e c h o.

And she soon realised that her
**house** simply wasn't a **home**
when it was just four walls.

e c h o

e c h o

e c h o

Three collected creepy-crawlies
in her underground cave.

But she had to admit they weren't
the most interesting company.

And soon she found that her
house simply wasn't a home when
it was just some windows.

Four went to parties.

But he didn't know anyone and the people weren't very friendly.

It was as if they had never seen a badger boogie-woogie before!

And, sure enough, he quickly learned that a house simply wasn't a home when it was just a floor.

All the **not-so-best** friends were sad and lonely.

They missed their **house** that was a **home**.

But most of all,
   they missed each other.

Something had to be done.

"I'm sorry," said One.

"Me too," said Two.

"Me three," said Three.

"Me four," said Four.

The best-again-friends had a big hug,
and then they set about fixing their house. . .

. . . until it was a home once more.

But they decided to add
something new:
something which meant they
could all go to the seaside . . .

and they could all learn to yodel on the
top of a mountain . . .

and they could all collect bugs in the
deepest, darkest caves . . .
and they could all go to the
poshest parties in the big city.

"Now we can go everywhere together!" they said.

And they did.